Shh!
Can you
keep a secret?

You're about to meet the
Ballet Bunnies, who live hidden at
Millie's ballet school.

Are you ready?

Tiptoe this
way. . . .

Meet the Ballet Bunnies

Dolly

You'll never meet a bunny who loves to dance as much as Dolly.

Fifi

If you're in trouble, Fifi is always ready to lend a helping paw!

Pod

Pod loves to build things out of the bits and pieces he finds. He also loves his tutu!

Trixie

Yawn! When she's not dancing, Trixie likes curling up and having a nice snooze.

For Serenie Beans

Text copyright © 2021 by Swapna Reddy
Cover art and interior illustrations copyright © 2021 by Binny Talib

Visit us on the Web!
rhcbooks.com

Educators and librarians, for a variety of teaching tools, visit us at
RHTeachersLibrarians.com

Library of Congress Cataloging-in-Publication Data is available upon request.
ISBN 978-0-593-30575-1 (trade) — ISBN 978-0-593-30576-8 (lib. bdg.) —
ISBN 978-0-593-30577-5 (ebook)

MANUFACTURED IN CHINA
10 9 8 7 6 5 4 3 2 1
First American Edition 2022

This book has been officially leveled by using the
F&P Text Level Gradient™ Leveling System.

Random House Children's Books supports the First Amendment
and celebrates the right to read.

Ballet 🐰 Bunnies

The Big Audition

By Swapna Reddy

Illustrated by Binny Talib

A STEPPING STONE BOOK™

Random House 🏠 New York

Chapter 1

"Watch MEEEEE!" Fifi cried.

The little bunny swung from the low-hanging branches of the weeping willow tree. She let go of the branch and flew into a grand jeté, before landing in the soft grass by Millie.

"Oh, bunny fluff!" Pod exclaimed, his

long velvety ears standing tall. "I want to try that!"

Millie giggled as she watched her four tiny bunny friends hop toward the low branches, all eager to fly through the air.

For you and me, four talking, dancing bunnies swinging from a willow tree into grand jetés might seem a little odd. But for Millie, hanging out with the Ballet Bunnies from Miss Luisa's School of Dance was just another Saturday in the park.

"I have exciting news," Millie said as the bunnies bounced into a fluffy heap in the grass.

Dolly, Fifi, Trixie, and Pod hopped up onto Millie's lap as she leaned in close to talk to them.

"*Ballet Beat* is filming at Miss Luisa's school next week!" Millie squealed.

Millie and Mom loved *Ballet Beat*. It was their favorite TV show. They would cozy up on the couch to watch the famous dance show together every Sunday evening. They oohed and aahed over the sparkly costumes and the incredible acrobatic routines showcased each week.

"They're filming children from different dance classes for the very first time," Millie continued, "and they are looking for someone from *my* class to appear on the show!"

The bunnies looked up at Millie, wide-eyed with excitement.

"You would be amazing on that show," Pod said. "They *have* to choose you."

The bunnies nodded in agreement, but Millie shook her head.

"I'm not good enough to audition," Millie said.

"You won't know until you try," Trixie said.

Millie made a face.

"Trixie's right," Dolly agreed.

Millie made another face. "I don't know," she said slowly.

Seeing Millie's hesitation, Pod hopped

up onto her shoulder. "What did your mom say?"

"I haven't told her I'm not going to audition," Millie admitted.

"It might be a good idea to tell her how you feel," Pod said gently.

Millie nodded. If anyone knew how much this would mean to Millie, it would be Mom.

Chapter 2

Millie got ready to pack up the mini picnic that she had set up for the bunnies. Then she stopped.

"Hang on," Millie said, looking down at the bunnies. "How come you don't seem surprised to hear about *Ballet Beat*?"

The four bunnies grinned at each other.

"We already knew!" Dolly squealed.

"What?" Millie gasped. "How?"

"It's the talk of all the dance schools in town," Fifi said.

Pod clapped his paws in excitement. "Everyone's so excited about it."

"*Everyone?*" Millie asked.

"We heard from the Ballet Bunnies at the dance school by the train station, and *they* heard from Ballet Bunnies at the small studio by the mall," Trixie piped up.

Millie's mouth hung open. *There were more Ballet Bunnies?*

"Oh, bunny fluff," Dolly said to the

others. "I think Millie thought we were the *only* Ballet Bunnies around."

The bunnies giggled as Millie shook her head in disbelief.

"We probably shouldn't mention the Hip-Hop Hedgehogs and the Mambo Mice, then," Fifi whispered cheekily.

"Or the Bhangra Blue Jays," Pod said with a grin.

"I know all about bhangra," Millie blurted out. "My friend Samira taught me some moves."

She whipped up her arms in the air, then shrugged her shoulders in time to the beat that Pod tapped out with his paws. Dolly, Fifi, and Trixie joined in, jumping next to Millie.

The bunnies stomped along until they were all exhausted, and they collapsed in the grass.

"You know, you could meet the rest of the Ballet Bunnies if you wanted!" Dolly suggested.

"Really?" Millie said as she caught her breath. "The others wouldn't mind?"

"Of course they wouldn't mind," Fifi said. "We've told them all about you, and they can't wait to meet you."

Millie blushed. She couldn't quite wrap her head around the idea that every dance studio had its very own family of Ballet Bunnies. Or Hip-Hop Hedgehogs or Mambo Mice or Bhangra Blue Jays for that matter.

Dolly bounced up into Millie's arms. "We're having a talent show, here in the park, to celebrate *Ballet Beat* coming to town," Dolly said to Millie. "And you can be our guest of honor."

Chapter 3

Millie tugged at Mom's hand as they left the park for the dance school.

"Mom! Everyone is so excited about *Ballet Beat* coming to Miss Luisa's school," Millie said.

"Are you excited?" Mom grinned.

Millie nodded, but Mom could see something was bothering her.

"Is everything okay, Millie?" Mom asked.

Millie took a deep breath. She remembered that Pod had said she should talk to Mom about her worries.

"There's going to be an audition, and they're only going to pick one person, and I'm not sure I'm good enough," Millie blurted out.

"Oh, Millie," Mom said, hugging her close.

Millie wrapped her arms around Mom tight. "I'm not sure I'm as good as everyone else in my class," she whispered.

Mom pulled away gently and gazed down at Millie. She smoothed back the stray strands of hair that had escaped from Millie's bun.

"All anyone can ask of you and all you can ask of yourself is to do your very best," she said to Millie. "I know how hard you're working at ballet. And I know how much you love it. Give yourself a chance to show everyone how ballet makes you feel."

When Millie was dancing, there was no better feeling in the world.

Mom smiled, and Millie felt all her fears melt away. Mom was right. Millie would try her hardest, and no matter what might happen, she would always know she had done her best. That thought made her feel very proud.

◦ ✳ ◦

Miss Luisa showed the class the routine for the audition. It was more difficult than anything they had ever been taught, but the whole class was excited to learn. Millie was very impressed with everyone, especially Will. She couldn't help but stop to admire Will's clean spins and effortless jumps.

"He's so good," Samira said, pausing next to Millie at the barre.

"I know!" Millie said. "I can't wait to dance like that."

"Neither of you will ever dance like that if you just stand around talking." Amber

smirked as she spun past them. "Now move! You're in my way."

Amber had never been very nice to Millie, but today she was in a particularly mean mood.

"There's plenty of space to practice, Amber," Samira said, waving her arms around.

"This class should be for those of us who *actually* stand a chance of getting chosen for *Ballet Beat*," Amber snarled. "Those of you who would never make it should go and chat somewhere else," she added, looking down her nose at Millie and Samira.

"Ignore her," Samira said, squeezing

Millie's hand as Amber pirouetted off to the other side of the studio.

Millie gave Samira a small smile. She wanted to ignore Amber's comments, but they hurt.

Chapter 4

At the end of class, Millie grabbed her things and left the studio to wait for Mom in the entryway, where she noticed Amber in a corner.

As Millie stepped closer, she saw Amber's face fall. She recognized Amber's mom's voice. Amber and her mom were

talking, but neither of them looked
very happy at all.

"No, you can't go to your friend's house tonight," Amber's mom said.

"But—" Amber started.

"Or any other night, for that matter," Amber's mom continued, her voice rising. "You will be practicing every night until the day of the audition. Do you understand, young lady?"

Amber's shoulders hunched forward, and she hung her head. And though Millie couldn't quite see, she thought that Amber was crying.

"I don't want to hear any more of this," Amber's mom went on. "You *will* get that part. Do you hear me?"

"But what if I don't?" Amber said, her voice small.

"That's enough, Amber. We've spoken about this, and there's no excuse for failure," her mother replied. She turned on her heel and grabbed Amber's ballet bag. "I'll see you by the car."

Amber's mom brushed past Millie and strode out the doors.

Amber was still staring at her feet as she wiped away tears from her wet cheeks. When she looked up, she saw Millie offering her a kind smile.

"What are you looking at?" Amber scowled, sticking out her chin and storming off after her mom.

Chapter 5

On the way home, Millie asked Mom if she could play in the park. It was still light out, and Mom wanted to catch up with her friends too. Millie and Mom sprinted all the way to the swings, pretending to be super-speedy race cars.

Mom spotted Mrs. Singh and they started chatting, so Millie headed over to the willow tree, where she knew the Ballet Bunnies would be rehearsing for their big show.

Millie's encounter with Amber disappeared from her thoughts as soon as she saw Dolly pirouetting across the grass. The little bunny danced to the melody Fifi played on a tiny recorder she had crafted out of a matchstick.

"Millie!" Pod called as she approached. "Watch my magic trick."

Pod swung his little magician's cape around his body. He held it out in front of him so just his ears peeked over the top.

"Three, two, one . . . ," he counted.

The cape dropped.

And Pod had completely disappeared!

Millie gasped. *Where was Pod?*

He reappeared and laughed when he noticed Millie's mouth hanging open in wonder.

"How did you do that, Pod?" Millie asked.

"It's supposed to be a secret," Pod said. His nose twitched as he beckoned Millie closer. "Don't tell anyone," he whispered. "But I run as quickly as I can before the cape drops so it looks like I vanish into thin air!"

"That's such a great idea," Millie said, applauding Pod.

Trixie, who had been dozing in a shady spot, hopped over to join them.

Millie stroked Trixie's velvety fur. "What will you be doing for the talent show?" she asked the tiniest of the four bunnies.

The sleepy bunny yawned. "My special skill is napping."

Millie chuckled as Trixie squeezed

herself into a teacup, and then onto a large fern frond, and then into a pencil case, showing that she could, in fact, sleep absolutely anywhere.

All four bunnies gathered together as Millie cuddled them in a big snuggly hug. She nuzzled into their soft fur and gave their long silky ears a stroke each.

"How was class today?" Dolly asked. "We were so busy rehearsing for the talent show that we didn't make it to the school."

Millie told them all about the new routine and how exciting it was to try something more challenging. As she spoke, Millie's smile turned into a frown. She remembered Amber's mean words, and she told the bunnies what had happened with Amber and her mom.

"It sounds like she has a lot to prove to her mom," Fifi said.

"It's no excuse for being mean, though," Dolly said.

The bunnies agreed. Before anyone

could say anything more, Mom called for Millie. Hearing her mom's voice and seeing the bunnies around her, Millie felt very lucky to have the support she had.

◦ ✳ ◦

"I have something for you," Mom said, plonking down on the grass next to Millie. The bunnies had darted behind the willow tree before Mom could spot them.

Mom handed Millie a package wrapped in a green ribbon.

Millie tore off the ribbon. She pulled open the box and peered in.

It was a new pair of tights and ballet shoes.

"Mom! They are just like the ones Precious has," Millie said, thinking of her favorite ballerina of all time.

"I want you to know, no matter what

happens in the audition, you have already made me so proud," Mom said. Millie hugged her.

Millie couldn't wait. She slipped on the tights and shoes right there and stretched out her legs. At that moment, she felt like a professional ballet dancer.

She squeezed Mom tight again, and as she kissed her, she saw her four Ballet Bunny friends grinning up at her from behind the tree. Millie felt her chest fill with warmth. She couldn't wait to work hard on her audition and show off her dancing in her beautiful new shoes.

Chapter 6

Millie tapped her feet on the wooden floor. It was audition day. She had on her new tights and shoes, and she couldn't stop gazing down at them. She'd spent the last few days working really hard on her audition. She danced for Mom. She danced for the Ballet Bunnies. She

danced for her neighbor, Mrs. Singh. She even danced on the way to the store. Millie danced any chance she could get.

Mom had dropped her off at the town hall, where the auditions were taking place. Dolly had snuck into Millie's ballet bag to come along too. Millie and Dolly watched the hall fill with young dancers. They stretched and warmed up, and the low din of chatter started to get louder in the hall. Millie felt a flurry of nerves grow and swirl in her tummy.

"You'll be fine," Dolly said, spotting Millie wringing her hands.

Millie managed a small smile, but she didn't feel fine.

Millie and Dolly watched as Will was called to the dance floor. He soared through the air and pirouetted with perfection. Will was good. He was really, really good. Millie desperately wanted to watch her classmate finish his routine, but the more she watched, the more her tummy hurt. *Could she ever dance as well as Will?*

Dolly tapped Millie with her paw. Her nose twitched toward an empty corridor that opened off the main hall. Millie scooped up the little bunny, and they left Will's audition to head out to the quiet hallway.

"Is everything okay?" Dolly asked once they were alone.

Millie started to nod, but it quickly turned into a shake of her head.

"It's so big," Millie said. "It's not like Miss Luisa's studio at all."

The high ceilings and huge open space of the town hall made an excellent audition spot, but it felt cold and intimidating, nothing like Miss Luisa's cozy studio.

"It's just another place to dance," Dolly reassured Millie. "It's just another place to fill with your love for ballet."

Dolly jumped out of Millie's hands and dove into Millie's ballet bag. She rummaged around inside before hopping back out to join Millie.

"Remember when you first joined Miss Luisa's school?" Dolly said. "It was difficult, and you weren't sure you wanted to keep dancing," she continued. "And do you remember that we talked about how ballet made us feel like we were flying across clouds of cotton candy?"

Millie smiled. She did remember. She remembered struggling to keep up with the class at first. She remembered that when she was just about to give up, the ballet steps made sense and she felt like she was flying when she danced. She remembered finally making friends and how much she loved ballet.

"I got you this," Dolly said.

She handed Millie a small hair clip, decorated with a small tuft of pink tulle.

"It's the cotton candy hair clip you made me!" Millie exclaimed.

She slipped the clip into her hair and touched the fabric gently.

"Don't worry about what happens today," Dolly said. "Just go out there and dance like you are flying over cotton candy!"

Chapter 7

It was time for Millie's audition.

She took a deep breath and stepped out into the center of the hall. She reached up to squeeze her hair clip and felt a burst of warmth in her chest. She knew, tucked

away in a corner of the hall, Dolly would be watching and cheering her on.

One of the judges counted Millie in, and the audition music sounded. Millie took another deep breath and placed her feet in first position.

The rhythm flowed through Millie like paint on an easel. As the music built, Millie's nerves melted away to nothing. She spun and jumped and pirouetted and did pliés, just like Miss Luisa had taught her.

Her ballerina dress floated around her like a silk ribbon in the wind. Millie soon forgot anyone was watching as she twirled faster and faster to the music. She couldn't help but smile the whole way through as she felt each note from the bottom of her toes all the way up to the tips of her fingers. And as she took her final jump, she soared through the air like she was flying over cotton candy.

Millie curtsied as the music died down. She saw the judges beaming at her, and in that moment, she felt so proud of herself. She had remembered her steps and she had done her very best.

Millie stepped to the side as the judges made their notes, and she saw that Amber was next.

Amber had her arms wrapped tight around herself. Her skin was pale, and she was trembling. Millie had never seen Amber like this. Amber was nervous.

"Good luck," Millie said, smiling at her. She reached out to offer a comforting hand, but Amber pushed past her without even so much as a thank-you.

Chapter 8

Millie watched as Amber finished her routine, curtsied, and then dashed off toward an empty hallway. Millie followed her.

"Amber?" Millie called out.

Muffled sobs were the only reply.

Millie followed the sound. She found

Amber huddled in a corner, behind a stack of chairs. She was crying into her knees.

"Are you okay?" Millie asked, crouching down to sit close to Amber.

Amber shook her head, so Millie searched her own bag for a spare tissue and offered it to her.

Amber looked up. "Why are you being nice to me? I'm not very nice to you."

Millie shrugged. "You look really upset."

Amber brushed away the tears from her wet cheeks. "I wish I'd done better in my audition."

Millie looked confused. "But you were really good."

"I don't think I was good enough," Amber said, her voice small. "And if I don't get the part, my mom will be really disappointed in me."

"I don't think she will," Millie said gently. "I saw your audition. It was really, *really* good. I could tell you were trying your hardest."

Amber curled up tighter into a ball but kept her eyes on Millie.

Millie remembered what her mom had said to her. "All anyone can ask of you is to do your very best," Millie said to Amber. "You showed everyone out there how much you love ballet, and that's all that matters."

"I did," Amber said, her voice still tiny.

"You should tell your mom how you feel," Millie continued.

"I don't think she'll understand," Amber said, weeping.

"You won't know unless you try," Millie said. She put her arm around Amber's shoulder and gave her a squeeze.

Amber took a deep breath. She swallowed hard and nodded.

She sat up straight, pushed back her shoulders, and wiped her tears away.

Then, she put her arm around Millie and gave her a squeeze back.

"Thank you, Millie," she said, sounding a little more like the confident Amber that

Millie knew. Amber took Millie's hands. "I'm really sorry for being mean to you."

◦ ✳ ◦

Millie sat with Mom, holding her hand tight, as the audition results were announced. She felt in her pocket for Dolly, who nuzzled back reassuringly.

Neither Millie nor Amber got the part. It went to Will.

Amber gave Millie a small smile and shrugged when the *Ballet Beat* judge called Will's name. Millie watched from across the hall as Amber spoke to her mom. Millie felt a warmth in her chest again, like summer sunshine, when she saw Amber and her mom hug each other.

"Are you okay?" Mom asked Millie.

Millie nodded, though she couldn't help but feel a twinge of disappointment in the pit of her tummy.

"I'm so proud of you," Mom said, hugging Millie tight. "I think we deserve a trip to the park."

Chapter 9

"Oh, bunny fluff," Fifi said as Millie and Dolly joined them in the park. "You deserved that part, Millie," she said.

"It's true," Dolly said. "You danced just as wonderfully as Will, so they could have easily picked you, Millie."

Millie smiled. She *had* danced her best, and as she thought back to her audition, she realized just how proud she was of herself.

"There will be lots of other parts to audition for," Pod reassured her.

"You are the best bunny friends anyone could ask for," Millie said.

She scooped them up in a huge hug and placed them down by a small stage set up beneath the willow tree.

Red cloth napkins had been tied up to make curtains, and smooth, flat stones had been set out in front of the stage as seats for the audience.

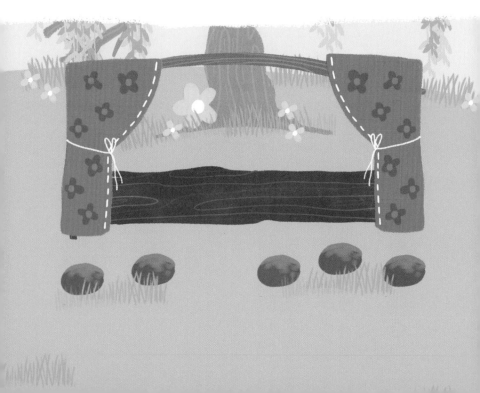

Fifi and Pod couldn't wait to introduce Millie to all the Ballet Bunnies and Mambo Mice and Hip-Hop Hedgehogs and Bhangra Blue Jays. Millie had to repeat everyone's name twice to remember all the wonderful new dancers she'd just met.

"I'd better get to my seat," Millie said to everyone. "Your talent show is about to start!"

She wished each of them good luck and sat under the willow tree ready to watch the show.

Pod started the show with his vanishing trick. Even though Millie knew exactly what was going to happen, she couldn't help but gasp with the others when his cape dropped and he reappeared in the audience by the Hip-Hop Hedgehogs.

The Mambo Mice stunned everyone with their complicated dance routines and their glittery outfits. The Bhangra Blue Jays had everyone up on their feet, paws, and claws with a bhangra class to start off their routine.

But it was Dolly who stole the show.

Her ballet routine was utterly magical. She danced like she was painting a picture with her movements, sweeping the entire audience under her spell. And when Dolly was announced as the winner, Millie leapt to her feet with the other animals and cheered louder than anyone.

Dolly hopped straight over to Millie after she collected her trophy—a G clef carved from a fallen branch.

"I'm so proud of how hard we have both worked this week," she said to Millie.

"Me too," Millie said, her chest swelling with pride.

Twirl and spin with the Ballet Bunnies in these adventures!

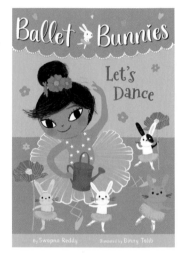

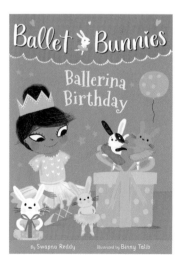